I0764585

101 TWISTED TALES

Dinesh Singh is a man of many parts—mathematician, painter, educationist, public intellectual, acknowledged orator in English, Hindi and Urdu, and now a storyteller. A graduate of St. Stephen's College, Delhi, he obtained his doctorate from the Imperial College of Science, Technology and Medicine, London.

As the twenty-first vice chancellor of Delhi University, his ideas on education formed the backbone of his globally hailed reforms. These ideas are the cornerstone of the National Education Policy, 2020. Acknowledged globally as a distinguished mathematician and educationist, he has won several prizes as a mathematician and has been president of the Ramanujan Mathematical Society.

He is currently Vice Chairman of the Jammu & Kashmir Higher Education Council, a role in which he has introduced far-reaching reforms. He is also Distinguished University Professor at the O.P. Jindal Global University; Adjunct Professor of Mathematics at the University of Houston; and Chancellor, K.R. Mangalam University, Gurugram.

He has delivered public lectures at some of the world's most prestigious institutions, and has been honoured with the Padma Shri as well as several honorary doctorates from different countries.

101 TWISTED TALES

DINESH SINGH

Published by

Rupa Publications India Pvt. Ltd 2025
161-B/4, Gulmohar House,
Yusuf Sarai Community Centre,
New Delhi 110049

Sales centres:
Bengaluru Chennai
Hyderabad Kolkata Mumbai

Images credit: Krishangi Sinha

P-ISBN: 978-93-7003-452-5
E-ISBN: 978-93-7003-316-0

First impression 2025

10 9 8 7 6 5 4 3 2 1

Contents

FOREWORD

Shashi Tharoor

Unless it is one's own handiwork, it is rare to be involved in the production of a book from the very beginning. Similarly, only rarely does one feel that someone's creations must—absolutely must—be turned into a book. For it would, in fact, be selfish to keep them to oneself and deprive the world of a blazingly original, pioneering talent and its spellbinding creations. This would be an unforgivable sin—an affront to the majesty of literary creation. This sin cannot be committed. Not on my watch, at least.

But worry not, dear reader. The majesty of literary creation is alive and kicking. We are not in sin. For you are holding in your hands—I am pleased to note—Dinesh Singh's *101 Twisted Tales*. I may have, as the Gen Zs say these days, 'manifested' this moment. For no sooner had I read one of these stories and discovered that my friend—the former vice-chancellor of the University of Delhi—had a penchant for composing stories that could be read in one breath, than I began prodding him not only to write more, but also to turn them into a book—one apt to fly off the shelves as soon as it is stocked. Now, I know that having written a sentence as long as the preceding one—and this one is getting rather long too!—I run the risk of losing

Dinesh, the author of the pithy sentences that follow, as a friend. Nevertheless, I shall take this risk. He may be able to spin entire yarns with a few flourishes of his pen. But I need my time (and, if necessary, multi-clause sentences) to explain what a seminal talent he is and how stunning his achievement is.

As professor at, and later vice-chancellor of, Delhi University, Dinesh has spent many long years surrounded by youngsters, teaching and guiding them. In the process, he has become a youngster at heart himself. Hence his ability to write for all ages. To endear himself to both the young and old. But more important, finding himself at the centre of an eternal eddy of students, swirling about him day in and day out, brought him face to face with a depressing leitmotif of our dizzyingly digitized times—a declining attention span.

'In the future,' quipped Andy Warhol, the maverick American artist and leading light of pop art, 'everyone will be world-famous for fifteen minutes.' I do not know about fifteen minutes of success, but fifteen seconds of attention are definitely what characterize our world—most of whose denizens are incorrigibly online, doomscrolling on a bountiful buffet of social media sites—in the third decade of the twenty-first century. Observing this phenomenon up close—of Gen Z (and, increasingly, even the older generations, the millennials and boomers) tumbling into the addictive black hole, as endless as it is (paradoxically) ephemeral, of seconds-long Instagram reels, YouTube shorts, and TikToks—Dinesh seems to have stumbled on an incisive realization. Just as the means and duration of imbibing information and being entertained—consuming 'content', in other words—have changed, so too must our ways of narrating stories. Ours, after all, is the age of Twitter (now X), where earlier in 140 characters, and now in 280 characters, war can be proclaimed and peace brokered, love can be professed and hatred mobilized, information can be shared and misinformation peddled. Today, in other words, everything is possible in a few hundred characters and a couple of sentences, including storytelling. Thus, you have Dinesh's tantalizing 'twitterstory'.

This, he explains in his preface, is so short as to be encased in 'a single tweet on the social media platform X.' Moreover, 'each story ends with an unexpected twist,' which never fails to make our eyes widen in surprise or bring a smile—at times wry, at times warm—to our face. Above all, as you read these tiny tales, composed with inimitable deftness, you cannot help being in awe of the author's colossal breadth of knowledge and expansive, all-embracing humanity. As Dinesh rightly points out, 'these stories, though very short, manage to evoke varied human emotions in the reader. Several of these are quite funny, some of them intrigue and some evoke a kind of reflective sombreness.'

Dinesh labels the form of these Twitter stories a

'prosaic counterpart to the haiku,' the crisp Japanese poetry style of seventeen syllables, structured in three lines of five, seven and five, traditionally deployed for conjuring visuals of the natural world. The form and style of Dinesh's sagas, however, are far more subversive than merely being a 'prosaic' equivalent of an extant style. For he has attempted to encapsulate the stories and histories, adventures and anxieties, trials and tribulations, of our perpetually online world in a format we understand (and, in many ways, articulate ourselves in) best—the 140- to 280-character range of an X post. In my view, to an age beleaguered by a lack of attention, and which has fallen head over heels for short-form content, Dinesh has gifted a brave new style of storytelling. As he himself writes, 'in crafting these so very short stories, I may well have engendered a whole new genre of short stories...'

I found Dinesh's spirited attempt at rewriting the rules of storytelling impressive. In discussing my own fiction, I have long argued that as the very word 'novel' suggests, there must be something innovative about every book I set out to write. It is not a novel that Dinesh has written, but I have no doubt that he shares my conviction that there must always be something novel—something bold and enticing—about the very act of storytelling. After all, in *The Thousand and One Nights*, the razor-sharp Scheherazade managed to keep herself and her sister, Dunyazad, alive not by narrating to King Shahryar plain, old tales in a dreary manner, but by entrancing that murderous, misogynistic sovereign with a succession of sagas whose entwined, endless and exhilarating frame structure prevented the sisters from meeting a grisly end.

As I perused the final proof of this volume, mesmerized beyond words by these playful and poignant tales, luminous in their brevity, I wondered whether there is an English equivalent of the Hindi phrase '*gagar mein sagar*'. Translating to 'an ocean in a pitcher', this expression is primarily used for poetry, to convey the idea of immeasurable beauty and wisdom captured in short form—and breathtakingly at that. This really is the only way of describing Dinesh's creations, which enfold whole worlds, epochs and lives into a few short, scintillating sentences. Yet, a nagging voice within me demanded, what is the English counterpart to this Hindi saying? Almost instantly, the opening line of William Blake's *Auguries of Innocence* sprang to my mind, and I found my answer—and an equally apposite way of describing my friend's stories: 'to see a world in a grain of sand'. So ultimately, through the sagas in *101 Twisted Tales*, as sparkling as they are succinct, Dinesh Singh reveals to us entire worlds in grains of sand. In the process, he empowers us to reimagine, as he has, the wonder and fragility of life on this pale blue dot, where our stories—and perhaps even our very existence—may well be hanging by a thread of over a few hundred characters.

PREFACE

This book is a collection of very, very short stories; so much so that each one of them fits inside a single tweet on the social media platform X. Each story ends with an unexpected twist and that endears the stories to all and any who have had occasion to read them. In crafting these so very short stories, I may well have engendered a whole new genre of short stories as a sort of prosaic counterpart to the haiku. I have chosen to christen this form Twitterstory. However, this is not what makes the stories special or unique. It is the manner in which these extremely short stories have been crafted that makes them stand out, because then they strike an emotional chord in almost everyone who has had occasion to read them. Interestingly, the number of such folk who have been reading and commenting on so many of these stores is large enough to constitute a sound and diverse feedback platform—and it is this feedback that fortifies my own conviction that there is merit in the collection. The feedback platform comprises lawyers, judges, parliamentarians, teachers, civil servants and students. In fact, over the last four years, I have used as a sounding board—for a number of these stories—two very large private chat groups of such folk that are quite active on a social media platform. Fortuitously, these two groups turned into a sort of fan base egging me on to write more of such stories. The same fan base has also urged me many a time to publish these in the form of a book.

Foremost amongst my friends, and one of the first to suggest that I put these stories in a book, has been my long-standing friend Shashi Tharoor. His urgings did much to give me delight and confidence and have made me look at my stories with greater affection. He has also penned a very generous foreword for the book. My other friends who have also repeatedly pressed me for a book are Chetan Seth, the always evocatively expressive cigar man; Arun Kapur the dynamic and visionary founder of educational institutions; Najeeb Jung, who has been an accomplished civil servant and a man of letters in the same measure; and my scholarly, wise and steadfast friends Ramu Damodaran and Kanwarjit Singh. My final conviction about the value of what I had crafted happened through my wife's young and gifted niece Krishangi—better known by her nickname Yami—when she gushed and fell in love with my stories. She has been my constant egger-on to help me finish selecting and honing my presentation. More importantly, she has designed evocative illustrations to significantly enhance the impact of each of the stories.

The upshot of all that has been said above is that eventually, and despite my various preoccupations, I sat down over many days to sort, collect and organize the outpourings of my digital pen. In doing so I also crafted some more. I am fond of each one of my creations, but I selected a short list of 101 from my collection. There is nothing very sacrosanct about the number 101 and I have several more such stories. While revisiting these creations, I have come to realize that there is one other feature—in addition to the fact that they end with a twist—that characterizes these stories as special. These stories, though very short, manage to evoke varied human emotions in the reader. Several of these are quite funny, some of them intrigue, and some evoke a kind of reflective sombreness. The stories are often connected with historical figures and often they are just plain fiction. And then, some are connected to human emotions and passions, while some render a peek into a world beyond humans. Some of the stories are philosophical even, but also relatable to our everyday existence. However, most of all, as so many of my young readers have said, the stories are very enjoyable.

Happy reading!

~1~

ALIBIS

I was in trouble with my boss. The situation seemed dire. Then a devilish thought flashed by. I decided to go directly to headquarters. I managed a fancy dinner with my boss' boss. My alibis were well rehearsed and they worked. My mother-in-law was pleased.

2

MAILA AANCHAL

The 'foreign returned' man asked in a reprimanding tone, 'why do you not wash your sari?' The peasant woman replied with candour, 'what shall I wear while it is washed?' The man, moved by compassion, forsook his upper garment for life. #mahatmagandhi.

~3~

ILLOGICAL

He was sinking into paranoia. He began to suspect his food was being poisoned. No amount of reasoning could work with him. He was irrational in the extreme.

Eventually, he starved to death. Gödel, the world's greatest logician, died of illogical behaviour.

4

A PRAYER

She knew it had happened in a well-known instance once earlier. In desperation, she made a fervent attempt along the same lines, hoping against hope. To her relief, she came down with the Spanish flu and died while her son recovered—Badshah Khan's wife and son.

5

AGONY

He loved her deeply over the years but was also distracted by work. He knew she yearned for his attention. He kept telling himself that his work would soon be done. Before he knew it, she fell for a young man. Too late. His daughter was gone. Fathers!

6

BARE TRUTH

Each day, I adorn myself and caress you with my eyes, but you scorn me. That slut smiles at you and you make her happy. Why do you not see the yearning in my eyes? I live in the perpetual hope that perhaps one day you will change. Lie to me just once; oh mirror!

7

REUNION

He was in the college cafe after 20 years. This married man had signalled his college flame for a rendezvous. She came and sat next to him. His pulse raced. Their hands touched; hesitantly at first. And then they kissed. Why not? She was his wife of 20 years.

8

BIGAMY

Joe was a ladies' man. Jill and Cathy were both madly in love with him and wanted to marry him. The indecisive Joe told them to sort it out. They suggested a bigamous union. Joe smiled and under the garb of visiting the restroom ran away to live with his mother.

9

CASANOVA

He was royalty indeed, by lineage and by persona. His demeanour in the prime of his adulthood never failed to impress the opposite sex. Their legs seemed to fail them. He treated them like he owned them. A feminist's nightmare had he not been a lion.

10

CODE BREAKER

This star mathematician, during WWII, cracked the Nazi enigma code without fuss. Then he cracked a tougher code that helped the war effort. All alone and in two weeks. No, not Turing. The Swede, Beurling, my mathematical progenitor; he shunned publicity.

~11~

FATE

The new PM was told by a sage that one of her sons was likely to suffer a political assassination and the other was likely to die in an air crash. She decided to discourage Rajiv from becoming a pilot and Sanjay from joining politics. The vagaries of fate.

12
THE STAR

She sat alone unnoticed in the lounge. At once school memories of evading night curfews and scaling walls rolled by. All to watch her 'dum maaro dum' on the silver screen. Here she was with silver hair. She could not see me with her one good eye. Bollywood dreams!

13
CONFESSION

'Father, I have sinned.' 'How so, my son?' 'I have spat on my mother; attacked her with instruments blunt and sharp; and tried to poison her. I have exploited my siblings for gain. Could I have angered her?' 'My son, she has answered you with Covid-19.'

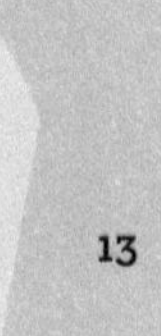

14
DISCHARGE

The old man confronted the visitor, 'Do you recognize me?' 'Yes,' he said. 'Do you recall your debt? 8 rupees 7 annas.' 'Of course.' 'I became a smoker because of you. Are your 'sams' still as good?' And Zia-ul-Haq handed Sukhiya 10,000 rupees on a visit to St. Stephen's.

15
DIVORCE

He married her on a whim. Over time he became unhappy. He deemed her listless and unable to converse and sought to engage a hotshot divorce lawyer. 'I cannot take up your case,' said the lawyer. 'But why?' he asked. 'Well, your wife has already engaged me.'

16

TRUE LOVE

She needed to bathe at the railway station. The first-class lounge had a bathing room. She had a third-class ticket. He let her use a friend's first-class ticket to access the restroom. 'My love for my wife overcame my love for truth.' #Gandhi #Kasturba

17

VAGABOND

As the shadows stretched, she waited, hoping he would come. At last he entered, and demanded 20 rupees. 'Sure, but why?' she asked, certain it was for a drink at the toddy shop. '10 to pay my fare and 10 to gift you for your rakhi.' Vagabond brothers!

18

WHY?

He was in despair. He wanted to be with his newly wed wife and tell her how much he loved her. She was upset. He found it hard to understand her distress. In any case, he was truly sorry and ready to apologize. After all, he was drunk when he had slapped her.

19

GRACE

My appreciation of Bollywood movies had something to do with her remarkable performances on the silver screen. Here I was—a trifle edgy—speaking publicly before her on a cold harsh day. But later, her graceful smile and words of praise lit up the 'mausam' for me.

~20~

GUILT

He warned his office staff about imagined slackness and used that as an excuse to deny them a bonus at Christmas. That day he felt good and gifted his mistress a diamond necklace. A gnawing guilt followed in its wake, so he bought a gold bracelet for his wife.

21

IN FLIGHT

This was the Briton's first trip by aeroplane. He had almost no money. The pretty stewardess asked twice to choose his dinner. He declined as he thought he had to pay. En route to Hollywood the first time. #SeanConnery

22

A DUEL

He was keen on her. She seemed unsure.

There was also this big guy; self-assured with a deep voice. He had to bring matters to a head. Seeing his chance, he lunged for the big one's throat who panicked and ran. He—Tommy—had won her heart; for her tail wagged.

23

GRIT

The rules were stacked against the cyclist. A daunting route that puts the Tour de France to shame. No drugs. No helmet. No kit. Nothing but the cyclist's armour of grit. Of course her papa was with her; a motivating burden. #rescue #Delhi-to-Bihar #Covid

24

INFATUATION

At 16, this was infatuation in the extreme. He would stare secretly at her from his room across the wall. One day, he found her standing all alone. He jumped the wall and mounted her from behind. 'I see you like my Enfield,' said the neighbour.

25

INTERVIEW

The newly arrived bar-at-law from London badly needed the English language teacher's job in the Bombay school, but was rejected. 'I have qualified at the bar in London and my English is good.' 'Yes, but you are not a graduate, Mr M.K. Gandhi.'

26

INVADER

His undefeated and marauding army was amassed across the river, ready to invade a defenceless Europe. Then, an old man rode over on a donkey and had a private conversation with him. No one knows what was said but the invader turned back. #AtillaTheHun #PopeLeo

~27~

IRONICAL

1981. John—a talented math kid—brazenly advised Kit—an average student—to not waste his life on math. I was friends with both and had agreed with John. In 1985, Dr Kit became a professor at Oxford and John killed himself after failing his PhD exam.

28

GUNPOINT

The somewhat masked man's gun was cocked and he wanted to 'loot' the treasure. His actions would enrich him beyond his dreams. There was tension in the air as the shooter pulled the trigger. This was one occasion when—as he fired—all applauded. #Olympics

29

KARMA

They were a couple in college. She was a foodie and he would spend all his money on feeding her. One day she vanished without a trace. He felt betrayed. Much later, he was on a flight and when the stewardess served him lunch, he smiled. That was her.

30

KHAMOSHI

She was seated in silence in the lounge. Having treasured so many images of her, I wished to ask about Guru Dutt, *Teesri Kasam*, Dev Anand and *Khamoshi*. Her graceful anonymity held me back. That very instant she turned to smile at me her silent thank you.

Silence

31

LARGE-HEARTED

The street vendor lady was obviously in need. On an impulse, I picked up an inexpensive pen, handed her a high-value currency note, and said, 'keep the change'. The lady smiled, took back her pen, and handed me a fancier pen instead.

Large-hearted indeed!

32

PROPOSING

I was madly in love and I proposed. She just smiled. I lived on hope for long and lost touch. And here she was with the same smile, asking 'will you marry me?' I mumbled and we laughed loudly. After all, 40 years ago she was 35 to my 5; my former KG teacher.

33
LIGHT

He had lost everything in the most unexpected of ways. Not even the most inveterate of gamblers could have kept composure against this card dealt by fate. Yet, he stayed the course to overcome the darkness and define the ethos of a nation. Happy Vijayadashami.

34

LOVE PANGS

Once there was a boy who loved this beautiful girl, but he was unable to express himself. He was a techie and so he brought me into play. I composed this paean to her. He bowled her over with my words: oh, how I wish I was human. #ChatGPT

~35~
MELTDOWN

He was a ruthless killer sent to get rid of this guy who would be easy to spot and kill on account of his sartorial style and gentle demeanour. The assassin went up to the 'mark', and stood face to face; and Angulimala fell at the Buddha's feet in surrender.

36

THE PAINTER

'Please, Giuseppe, why do you not paint my portrait? Am I not pretty enough?' But Giuseppe was adamant. 'Can you not see? My hands are full! But go over there to him. He will do a good job and he is free.' 'Are you sure?' 'Yes, Mona; Leonardo is good.'

37

MEMORIES

Many moons ago, I was in an apartment perched across from the leading lady of a Bimal Roy classic that had also starred Ashok Kumar. She beckoned, took my hand and kissed me, whilst the other lady in my life smiled. I was all of five years with my mom and N.

38

THE BOOK

As the train started, the young man commenced reading the book. He was deeply immersed in it and finished it just as his journey ended. He alighted from the train having found his mission. Ruskin's 'Unto This Last'. #Gandhi

39

VOWS

'She shall die from loss of blood but she stubbornly refuses meat,' said the surgeon. The young husband replied, 'I respect her decision.' 'Then leave my hospital.' The young man took her away. His love and faith nursed her to health. #Gandhi #Kasturba

~40~

MEN

He loved her with intensity. He was devoted to her and would spend much time with her. She too was interested and readily reciprocated his passion. Things were almost on a roll. There was just one glitch. If only his wife would understand. Men will be men.

41

STRANGER

Each evening, this fifty-ish man—unnoticed—ate a burger at a Mumbai McDonald's. One day, an elderly lady sat next to the man. Suddenly, she got up, stared at him and fainted. He smiled, 'This used to happen often when my *Kati Patang* was released.' #RajeshKhanna

42

PAYMENT

The enthusiastic barman was a hit at Jane's event. A lady guest asked him if Jane was going to compensate him well. 'No complaints,' said he. 'Jane shall let me sleep with her tonight.' What he did not tell the now wide-eyed lady was that Jane was his wife.

~43~

FEMME FATALE

He could not contain his physical desire for her. He knew the dues she would demand even as she wanted him too. Having sated his carnal needs, he blissfully paid the asked-for price to possess her and she—fulfilled and happy—killed him. #maleredbackspider

44

PANDEY

Its Ganga-Jamuni culture casts a spell over the Oudh region. It nurtures, beneath the land's laid-back life, a steely temper in the local folk. That steel propelled him to be hailed as the torchbearer of India's freedom struggle. #Mangal #martyr

45
NUPTIALS

He was going to spare no expense for his son's wedding. He had invited his entire world of friends and admirers. Came the day, a greater wedding was happening nearby. All roads were blocked. His invitees were stuck in their shanties, all eight of them.

46

THE MISTAKE

He looked exactly like James Bond from *Spectre*. He had his accent and mannerisms but when I asked him if he was James Bond, he said 'no' without batting an eyelid. I was walking away disappointedly when his lady friend said 'let's go, Daniel'. My mistake.

47
FANS

The senior gentleman waxed eloquent about his skipping college to watch Dilip saheb in *Ganga Jumna*. I turned to his wife and said that I had done something similar much later. She asked, 'And who did you watch?' Her eyes sparkled when I said, 'You, in *Guddi*.'

48

PALS

'I know at least half a dozen chaps who will readily qualify as my bosom pals.' My friend made this assertion to me in the hospital while being treated. 'How is that?' I asked. 'Well, look at my back. Six stab wounds made by six different blades.'

49

PLANS

He had chosen to retire and moved his library to his hometown. He was keen to write his autobiography. A ringside view of Indian politics. But the best-laid plans of mice and men... He was called–unexpectedly–to be anointed prime minister. #Narasimha_Rao

50

RAVAGES OF TIME

They were both at the college cafe at separate tables. The two lovers of an earlier era pretended not to recognize each other. A while later they departed.

He with his paunch. She with her arthritic gait. I sat watching with my girl the ravages of time.

~51~

BIG BANGS

She found herself facing a wooden partition, like a door. It was dark and she was scared witless. She screamed, banged, and knocked for the door to open. You would too if you were to wake up from a deep coma and find that you were about to be buried in a coffin.

52

REALITY

He had entered a joint venture in form and substance and had to adjust if he wanted to profit. He struggled to tell his partner to learn to do things the right way, but to no avail. Daily, the squeeze was from the top. Married life and toothpaste tubes.

53

THE VEGETARIAN

As the 'father' of his large household, he had imposed strict vegetarianism. Yet, when an esteemed non-vegetarian house guest arrived, he cooked meat for him. His acolytes were distressed. The 'father' remained unperturbed. #Gandhi #Badshah_Khan

54

REBEL

He was adamant on being a journalist. His father thought otherwise. 'You and your wife live under my roof. Do as I say. Be a lawyer.' The tussle was getting serious till a revered figure mediated to alter the course of history. #Nehru #Motilal #Gandhi

55

HEARTACHE

There were a million hearts that ached for her smile; all enslaved in the deep well of desire. They swayed and swooned in harmony with her heart. Alas, the burden of enslaving a million hearts took its toll. Her own heart gave way. #Madhubala

56

ROMANCE

He had been wooing her for long. He had tried every trick in the game, but to no avail. She seemed unsure and bashful. Then a brainwave hit him. He built a lovely home with a view for her on his property. Her heart melted and she moved in. His squirrel neighbour.

57

PASSION

The emperor asked the old man sternly, 'Will you stop uttering blasphemous things?' The old man responded, 'Why care what I say to my beloved?' 'And who is this beloved?' The old man turned his gaze gently skywards. The emperor then set Hazrat Nizamuddin free.

58

RULE BREAKER

He was strict about the rules at his hermitage. All meals were communal. Yet, when Sarla Debi visited, he dined with her privately. She had cast a spell on him, distressing his acolytes. He too was human, but he snapped out of it. #MahatmaGandhi

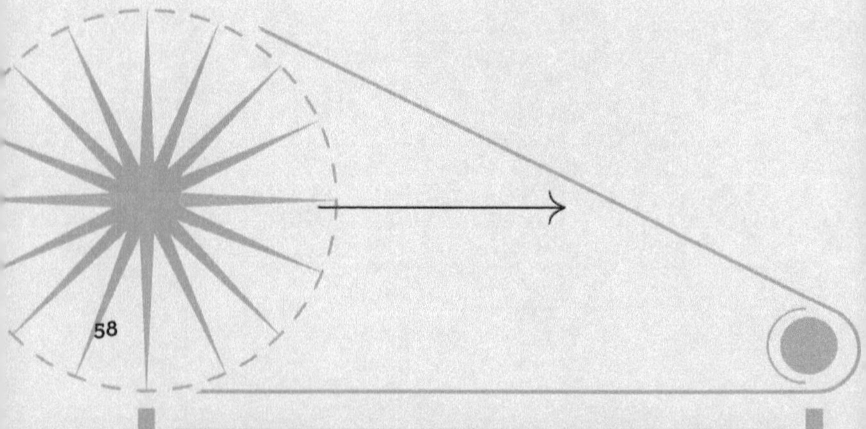

~59~

ASSASSIN

He stalked the 'mark' stealthily, his finger on the trigger, with a steely desire to kill. The first round had gone to the 'mark' who escaped after drawing his blood. Finally, the 'mark' was assassinated from behind. The electric zapper gave the mosquito no chance.

60

SAGE

He was successful beyond his expectations. It happened when he moved away from the moorings of his traditional upbringing. His abilities had been recognized somewhat. With supreme confidence, he now proffers advice for all problems back home. The #NRI syndrome.

61

SAVIOUR

He—a diehard vegan—came across a feline ready to pounce on a baby starling in a nest. His intervention saved the fledgling bird. Both, the bird and he, went to bed with contentment. Life plays strange games because three kittens went hungry that night.

62

SIN

Her smile was alluring but the stiletto-like thing in her hand was menacing. Smile or no smile, she meant to hurt me. My hands were clammy. Fear transfixed me. I prayed for salvation from my entrapment by bewitching chocolates, and for protection from dentists.

63

THE ERROR

She loved recounting how he boldly sent her a Valentine's Day card in college though they had not met. Flattered, she fell for him. They are now happily married. She is unaware he was actually courting a namesake. His card reached her in error. Lucky me.

64
POLLUTER

'May I bathe at your well?' asked the tired traveller. 'You may be low-born. I cannot risk that. My master shall return tomorrow and decide about your bath,' said the caretaker of the bungalow. At Patna—to Gandhi—before he commenced his historic Champaran visit.

~65~

TEST

Certain his wife was turning deaf, he decided to check. Walking towards her, he asked, 'Can you hear me?' He repeated the query twice and smiled upon hearing nothing each time. The smile faded as he got close and heard, 'My dear, that's the third time I said yes.'

66

DEBT

The struggling writer borrowed Rs 200 from the great poet. Later, the now-famous writer mentioned the debt. The poet said, 'Let the time come.' When the poet suddenly passed away, his gravedigger demanded Rs 200 from the writer. #SahirLudhianvi #JavedAkhtar

~67~

THE DIARISTS

They had agreed to keep a record of daily events. Her repeated entries read, 'He used cuss words all day.' It vexed him.

Then one day he wrote, 'Today she did not utter a single cuss word. I pray the same for tomorrow.' He slept soundly at night.

68

MISSES

He was happy when she told him on the phone: 'I missed you yesterday when you left home.' Obviously she was no longer upset, so he decided to return. As he entered, she smiled at him and said, 'I am not gonna miss again. I bought a much better gun.'

69

KIDNAP

At the London bus stop, she walked towards me seductively. My pulse raced as she perched herself beside me. Her alluring gaze overpowered me and soon, I found myself caressing her. I forgot my bus, hailed a cab, swept her off her feet and took her home. #cats

70

THE DOCTOR

A signboard beckoned patients for free treatment. Intrigued, I went in. An old man sat at a ramshackle desk. A radio was belting out old film songs. A popular Asha Bhosle number came on. Smiling he said 'my song'. The signboard said 'O.P. Nayar - homeopath'.

~71~

THE GOODBYE

He said bye as we parted and I failed to notice. I was distracted. Too much buzz in the air. Too much to savour. I was also careless. Of what avail now to hark to that goodbye of all goodbyes. Farewell to so many departed friends. Shall meet again.

72

HOMECOMING

Feted as royalty and sought by the world, this once famous figure had hosted all–the rich, the famous, and the rest–with grace and class. Then his fate nosedived and there seemed no redemption; but now he is back in the Tata fold. Hail the Maharaja. #AirIndia

~73~

THE LAME ONE

The tag 'lame one' had stuck indelibly. Did it matter to the 'lame one'? Vast territories were conquered by the lame one. All competition was decimated. The lame one was a source of awe and wonder for so many. Not for nothing, the king of mangoes: 'langda'.

74

REGRET

'I am sorry but there is no room for me to emote in the script. Drop the movie, my friends,' said the famed thespian. 'We think otherwise,' said the authors and made history by giving an unknown bloke a break. The thespian regretted forever at having rejected *Zanjeer*. #DilipKumar

75

PIETY

He was in the sanctum sanctorum of the famous shrine. With humility and devotion, he placed a single paisa as an offering, only to provoke the priest into cursing him. At once, he retracted it and probably never ever visited a shrine again. #MahatmaGandhi

76

THE RIVALS

'Anu, I saw you with him again last night.' 'But Jay, I want him as much as I want you.' 'Well then, I am the man in this home. I cannot allow this to continue. Choose between him and me.' 'Please do not do this. After all, he is as much your son as mine.'

77

THE SLEUTH

The famous sleuth was seated on a recliner, pipe in hand. I walked in and hastily handed my card. 'You live in GK, you are 43 years of age, and your father's name is Ashok.' His deductive prowess stunned me. Later, I noticed my Aadhaar card was missing.

78

HAUNTING

The large, isolated tamarind tree was said to be haunted by a spirit. Humans avoided it. As for me, I loved dreaming under the glorious silence of its shade. I thought of it as a friend. Alas, one day they chopped it down. Now its memories haunt me.

~79~

THE TIP

For $10, the Manhattan cabbie let me ride shotgun with him while he took other fares. A touristy lady hailed him. On a whim, I began to describe the sights around Central Park. She perked up with many queries. I did quite well for she tipped me $10 and planted a kiss.

80

THE WISEST

They came; his acolytes. They told him that he had been proclaimed as the wisest in the land by the oracle. Mystified, he sought the reason. At last he understood. He was the only one who knew that he did not know. #Socrates

~81~

UNION

They both walked up to the official—hand in hand—to get the world to formally recognize their union. The lovers had faced hurdles and even abuse in their journey. It was pure, passionate, unadulterated love. I know, for I presided at the wedding of Jill and Jane.

82

BIASED

He was losing his hearing but failed to recognize the fact. Once, in the middle of the night, he woke up laughing. His wife asked, 'A nice dream?' The next morning his diary entry said, 'My wife is losing her mind. She wanted ice cream at 2 a.m.' Men will be men.

83

UNLADYLIKE

While Rani's guests were enjoying the wine, she and Som were necking furtively. The pin in her brooch accidentally pierced his thumb. Later at dinner, she asked Som, 'How's your prick?' 'Red and swollen,' he responded. It was unladylike of Anu to spill her wine.

84

THE SAINT

The emperor commanded the famed guru to sing a hymn. He responded, 'Serving the whims of emperors takes me away from God.' The emperor, pleased at this candour, said, 'Ask for anything.' 'Don't send for me again,' said Kumbhandas. Akbar bowed with a smile.

85

VALUE

Mother and son stepped out of Harrods in a hurry. The son stopped to pay heed to the street musician on his violin. His mother smiled, 'Come, son. We can hear Joshua Bell at the Albert Hall tomorrow. Street violinists are a dime a dozen.' The violinist smiled. #Joshua #anonymous'

86

CLEVER

She and her estranged husband were living under the same roof. He had been defaming her cleverly on social media, in ways that were not liable. She was vexed till she finally retorted with this post: 'Yesterday my husband was not drunk and did not beat me up. Amen.'

87

THESPIAN

He thrived in the world of make-believe. The imagined world spurred his flights of fancy. He recreated the creations of others. Such a one should likely be dizzy forever. Not him. He was rooted in the realism of gentle love, kindness and wisdom. #Dilip_Kumar.

88

VIEW

From a Mumbai hotel, I viewed the tycoon's ugly high-rise via a telescope. The man–in the news for his son's lavish wedding–was humbly sweeping a balcony in a torn vest. 'Look!' I told my wife. 'Calm down,' she said. 'The scope is pointed at the adjacent slum.'

89

THE STAND-UP MAN

His acts had gone well with audiences. He connected with their funny bones. The audience liked him very much. Who does not wish to laugh? But his greatest act has been to make the world cry when he stood up to Russia for Ukraine. #Zelensky

90

WASHOUT

To avert nuclear war, an ultra-secure hotline had been installed in the White House. JFK was stealing a nap when it buzzed. He responded nervously, 'POTUS.' There was silence for a while. Then a voice said, 'Sorry, sir. I had dialled my laundry.' #truestory

91

OFFSPRINGS

The daughter was distraught. 'Dad says I cannot marry Jim as he is my brother and that you do not know.' 'Not to worry, go ahead and marry Jim,' her mom stated. 'But mom!' The mother was adamant. 'You are not Jim's sister. Take my word.'

92

WISDOM

'We admit only Brahmins,' said the sage to the lad of 12. The child responded, 'I know not my father, and my mother is low-born.' 'Child, a Brahmin is one who adheres to the truth. You are thus admitted. Enter.'
#Satyakama #Haridrumat #Upanishad

~93~

THE CONVICT

The 24-year-old was about to be hanged for murder. His parents were distraught. His father unearthed evidence that could have earned him a reprieve. But he issued a stern rejoinder: 'My death shall surely serve a greater cause.' #BhagatSingh

~94~

SANE

The VIP, on a visit to the asylum, found an inmate conversing on Kant. Finding the VIP sympathetic, the inmate narrated a tale of the conspiracy by his wife to have him committed, and sought his help. The convinced VIP turned to leave and was struck by a shoe on his head.

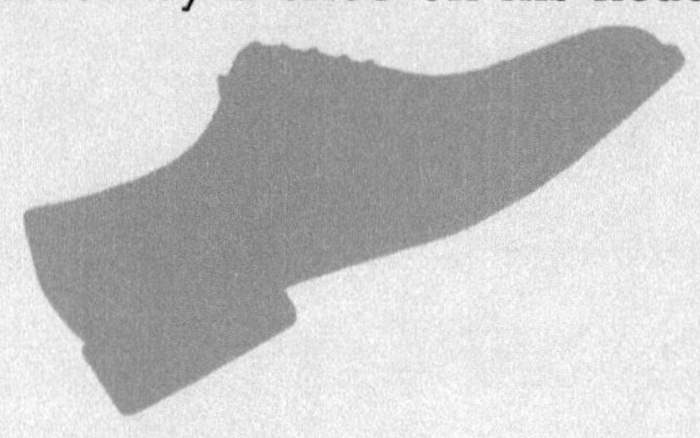

95

ISOLATION

The young man beseeched his shrink for help. 'I have this recurrent nightmare; I find myself—for no crime—sentenced to a long solitary confinement by a faceless judge.' The healer advised, 'To relax and feel free, I suggest to you, Robinson, a cruise so...'

96

FICKLE

One evening at Central Park, I sat on a bench already occupied by an elderly blonde. She was humming my favourite number from the 80s. I stared at her in disbelief and blurted, 'Fame is so fickle.'

She smiled back ruefully. #atomic #Blondie

~97~

WEAPON

Though Yudhishthira of the Mahabharata excelled in its use, it was not a fashionable weapon then, nor is it now. Yet, the young lad pierced the skies with it to quench the thirst for bullion of a billion people. Well done, son of India–Neeraj Chopra.

~98~

THE SEDUCTRESS

He got to know her in college. She seduced him in no time. In class, he would yearn for her and wanted her in bed. Aware that such passion was not good, he tried to dump her but failed time and again. He was in her grip. The allure of Lady Nicotine.

99

EGO

She heard a thump on her car window at the red light. A bedraggled and shivering old man was staring at her. On an impulse, she handed him a two thousand rupee note. She was upset that he failed to show appreciation for its value. Then her driver told her he was blind.

~100~

LOVERS

I was at the roadside bistro, and he was at the next table feeding his love interest with cake. He thought I wasn't looking and even stole from my plate. I almost protested but his unabashed affection held me back. And then they flew off. #sparrows

101

THE MATH PUZZLE

The pretty little thing's math teacher was an arrogant genius. Each time in class she said she couldn't follow, he would retort, 'Go sit on a rose bush.' Exasperatedly, she once asked, 'Why?' 'Well,' he said, 'if you do so, you'll soon get the point.'

www.ingramcontent.com/pod-product-compliance
Lightning Source LLC
Chambersburg PA
CBHW021621030826
48979CB00034B/522

* 9 7 8 9 3 7 0 0 3 4 5 2 5 *